Donnie was in his bedroom
looking out his window. Sweat
was running down his face and
his shirt.

Mary, Donnie's mom yelled,
"Why don't you go out and play
in the forest? It's too hot to stay
inside. Put on some shorts and
go see your animal friends."   2

Donnie went to the dresser
drawer, opened it and just
stared.   3

He went back to his bed and lied down staring at the ceiling.

One day Donnie wore shorts to school and you could see the big dark spot on his leg.

5

Donnie was remembering the incident at school. A group of boys came up to him and started to laugh at him. They pointed at the spot on his leg. 6

Donnie started to cry.

The teacher, hearing the noise, went over to the group of boys.

"Why are you crying Donnie?"
the teacher asked.

"These boys are laughing at the dark spot on my leg."

"I don't see anything funny about that. It's just a birthmark. It makes you unique," said the teacher.

"Boys, come with me to the principal's office now!"

The boys followed the teacher into the principal's office.

The teacher explained what happened. The principal listened and said, "This is a clear case of bullying, which means you unfairly picked on Donnie." 14

"As your punishment, you will each stay in time out today."

The boys left the principal's office with their heads hanging low.

On the bus ride home from school, no one sat next to Donnie.

Donnie, remembering what happened at school, began to cry.

Mary heard Donnie crying. She asked, "What's the matter?"

"I don't want to wear shorts.
I'm too embarrassed."

"Embarrassed about what?"
asked Mary.

Donnie replies, "This big dark spot on my leg!"

"Donnie, that's only a birthmark. There's no reason to be ashamed about that. I have an idea, come with me."

Mary took Donnie by the hand
and they went outside.

Mary walked with Donnie to the edge of the forest. They sat down.

25

Mary put her arm around
Donnie and pointed at the deer
in the distance. "See those deer?
They have spots on their bodies.
They are in all different places.
The deer are beautiful!"

"Look at Billy's dog. He has spots too. Everybody loves him."

"When you look at most animals they have some kind of marks or spots. That's what makes them unique. It identifies them and makes them special."

Donnie's eyes begin to light up. A smile comes to his face. "I'm just like my animal friends with my spot!"

"Yes, you are! You are very special. One of a kind and I love you for that."

"Mom, I want to go to my room and put on my new basketball shorts."

"I think that's a great idea. Let's go home so you can change." Mary started smiling.

Donnie went to the dresser in his bedroom and took out a new pair of shorts.

Donnie put on the shorts. He stood in front of his mirror and said out loud, "I am special!"